'He marched happily forward. It was only a hundred yards to his house on the other side of the road. He'd made it! The overgrown hedges and the tall, old gate posts at the ends of the drives welcomed him home.

Craig stepped out from behind the gate post of the first drive he came to. Jason's only thought was that it wasn't fair.

"I want you, Jason Peter Smith," Craig said coldly.'

Jason is in big trouble. Nasty, bullying Craig Sullivan is after him. Can Jason, with the help of his friends, find a way to stop Craig? Suddenly he has an idea . . .

BY MYSELF books are specially selected to be suitable for beginner readers. Other BY MYSELF books available from Young Corgi Books include:

YOUR GUESS IS AS GOOD AS MINE
    by Bernard Ashley
THE BIG RACE by Rob Childs
MIDNIGHT PIRATE by Diana Hendry
ALIX AND THE TIGERS
    by Alexander McCall Smith
THE AMAZING PET by Marjorie Newman
A GIFT OF SQUARES by Edel Wignell
A PUFF OF SMOKE by Catherine Sefton

JASON
AND THE
SCHOOL BULLY

Jason
and the
School
Bully

ERIC JOHNS

Illustrated by David Parkins

YOUNG CORGI BOOKS

JASON AND THE SCHOOL BULLY

A YOUNG CORGI BOOK   0 552 52497 2

Originally published in Great Britain by Young Corgi Books

PRINTING HISTORY
Young Corgi edition published 1988

This book is set in 14/18pt Century Old Style

Young Corgi Books are published by Transworld Publishers Ltd.,
61-63 Uxbridge Road, Ealing, London W5 5SA, in Australia by
Transworld Publishers (Australia) Pty. Ltd., 15-23 Helles
Avenue, Moorebank, NSW 2170, and in New Zealand by
Transworld Publishers (N.Z.) Ltd., Cnr. Moselle and Waipareira
Avenues, Henderson, Auckland.

Made and printed in Great Britain by
The Guernsey Press Co. Ltd., Guernsey, Channel Islands.

CHAPTER ONE

The Last Defeat Ever

Jason's Last Defeat Ever happened one day when the school bully stopped him on the way home. He would have been all right if the Pirates had been with him, but he had just said goodbye to them.

The Pirates were Ginny (which was short for Virginia), Josie (which was short for Josephine), Dan (which was short for Daniel) and Jason himself. He didn't shorten his name because it didn't shorten very easily. Also, he wasn't very tall and shortening anything about himself was not something he ever did.

They called themselves the Pirates because they lived by the sea in Coombe Bay and had an old boatshed as their den.

The Pirates were Jason's real friends. He also had one so-called friend, Alistair, who lived opposite him. He had to put up with Alistair because their mothers were friends and always said that the boys were too. Also, he felt a bit sorry for Alistair who didn't have any friends of his own.

Jason was with Alistair when the Last Defeat Ever happened. They had almost reached Jason's house when they heard whistling coming from behind. They looked round and saw Craig Sullivan cycling towards them.

'Pretend we've not seen him,' Jason whispered.

'He knows we have.'

'Just ignore him – or else.'

'Perhaps he won't stop,' Alistair said, not sounding very hopeful.

Craig had a gang of younger kids who followed him around and did whatever he said. They picked on anyone who was alone and made him hand over money or sweets or comics and threatened worse if reported.

Even Alistair had the sense to be afraid of him.

Craig rode past and turned to smile at them. He had a thin face but thick, pouty lips which made him look as though he was

sneering all the time.

'Hello, Craig,' Alistair said, trying not to give Craig an excuse to pick on him.

'What're you kicking?' Craig demanded.

'Nothing,' Alistair said quickly.

'You must be stupid kicking nothing,' Craig laughed at him.

Alistair laughed too. Jason tried to look as though he was thinking about something else. If he copied Craig, he'd be dragged into his army of slaves.

Craig swung his bicycle in a circle in the empty road.

'Shut up!' Jason hissed at Alistair, when Craig had his back to them. He rode up beside them again.

'That's a great bike,' Alistair said, giggling nervously.

Jason thrust his hands into his pockets.

He felt a pencil, string, shells from the beach, a penknife, last year's conkers.

'It's German,' Craig told them. 'Their bikes are better than the English ones.'

'How do you go so slowly?' Alistair asked.

'I've got a fixed wheel.'

'Can't you get it repaired?' Jason asked, to show that he didn't think the bike was so wonderful.

'You're a cheeky little dwarf, Jason.' Craig looked down at him from his saddle. 'What are you?'

'Dwarf sounds like a sort of animal,' Alistair said, giggling again.

'My dad says we all look like some animal.' Craig tossed his head to get his hair out of his eyes.

'What am I?' Alistair asked.

'Alistair the alligator,' Craig said, then added nastily, 'without any teeth.'

'What are you?' Jason asked before he could stop himself.

'My dad calls me tiger.'

'Sullivan the skunk,' Jason muttered.

Craig did not seem to hear. 'What is Jason, Alistair?' he asked. 'What about Jason the giraffe?'

Alistair laughed, hoping to please Craig. 'What's your other name, giraffe?'

'Smith,' Jason replied, feeling ashamed at saying his name.

'Smith's nothing. What's your middle name?' Craig asked with a sneering smile.

'I've not got one.'

'It's Peter,' Alistair told him.

'Peter the puppy,' Craig said, trying it out. 'Still not small enough.'

'He's got a panda at home.' Alistair knew everything about Jason.

'You wait,' Jason promised, clenching his fists round conkers and shells.

'Peter the panda,' Craig cried in triumph.

Alistair gave a shrill laugh.

'It's old,' Jason tried to explain, 'on top of a cupboard . . .'

'Do 'oo take your lovely pandy-wander to beddy-byes with 'oo?' Craig and Alistair slapped their sides, pretending to be helpless with laughter. 'Hey, Alistair, what do you think of this? Is it small enough? Peter the panda puppy! Panda puppy! Panda pup . . .'

Jason stretched out both hands and charged at the blurred shape on the bike. He could not stop the tears coming into his eyes and was furious at the thought that Craig might see them.

His charge took Craig by surprise, and he crashed down in the road.

'Now you've asked for it!' Craig yelled.

Jason saw the fuzzy shape of the bike on its side and, without thinking, jumped on

the spokes.

'Stop him, Alistair, you stupid fool!' Craig screamed, stuck half under his bike.

Alistair caught hold of Jason's arm and tried to drag him away. Then his foot slipped off the kerb, and Jason swung him round and flung him on top of the bike.

He threw the conkers and shells at them and ran.

'Wait till I get you, Jason. I'll kill you for this. Wait till tomorrow!' Craig shrieked, choking back sobs.

CHAPTER TWO

The Hunt Begins

The next morning Jason stayed in bed and pretended to be ill. He was too scared to go to school. His mother even said that he had a slight temperature.

Mark, his brother who was four years older, poked his head round the bedroom door. 'You look more horrible than usual,' he said and closed the door again before Jason could reply.

In the afternoon after school, Josie phoned up to find out what was the matter with him.

'Why weren't you at school today?' she asked.

'I've got a temperature,' he told her. 'Well, really I'm better now.'

'Can't you make it last another day?' Josie asked quickly.

'I suppose so. Why?'

'You want to keep out of the way,' she warned him. 'Did you know that Craig Sullivan was looking for you?'

'I thought he might be,' Jason said, glad that Josie couldn't see him over the phone. He had a sudden frightened feeling in his stomach and was sure his face showed how he felt. He could imagine Josie guessing everything and pushing her glasses back up her nose while she thought of what to say.

'What did you do to him?' she wanted to know.

'I pushed him off his bike.' Jason tried to sound tough. 'Then I jumped on his spokes – and bent them, I think.'

'He'll murder you,' Josie said in a hushed voice. 'Why did you do that?'

'He was picking on Alistair,' Jason said, half-truthfully.

'Poor old Alistair,' Josie said. 'I bet he was too frightened to be pleased at you helping him.'

'Yes. He tried to stop me,' Jason agreed. He heard a voice from Josie's end saying something.

'I've got to go and have supper,' she said. 'I'll tell the Pirates what's happened. See you on Friday if you can stay off. Watch out for Craig.'

'I will,' Jason promised.

'I think you're well enough for school,' Jason's mother said on Friday morning.

His stomach gave a jump. He wondered if he could stay away another day, then it would be the weekend. But he knew it was hopeless really. He got up slowly. Perhaps Craig wouldn't do anything. He might have forgotten.

'What's up with you?' Mark asked.

Jason had got as far as the bathroom and was standing as though turned to stone.

He swallowed. 'Nothing.' His voice sounded squeaky, even to himself.

'Yes, there is,' Mark insisted.

Jason wanted very badly to tell someone, even his brother, but he felt too ashamed to say that he was afraid to go to school.

'Tell you later, perhaps,' he said, trying to make his voice sound normal.

'Who're you afraid of?' Mark asked, seeing through his act.

'I don't know what you're talking about.'

'Is it old Evans at school?'

'No.'

'Jason's scared of Mr Evans,' Mark chanted, pushing past him into the bath-room and shutting him out.

'It's a lie,' Jason said, trying to sound angry but glad that Mark had not guessed the truth.

'Get a move on,' their mother called upstairs.

Jason slipped away to his room without washing. He felt sick.

Everything went more quickly that morning in spite of trying to do things in slow motion. Even the walk to school was somehow shorter than usual.

As he got near the school gates, every cyclist became Craig. He felt as nervous as on the first day.

'Hey,' a voice called, and he jumped.

'Oh, it's you,' he said, turning and seeing Josie. She had short, dark hair, always stood up very straight and was the fastest runner in their year. As usual, her glasses were halfway down her nose.

'Who did you think I was?' she asked him.

'Nobody.'

'Craig Sullivan Nobody, I bet,' she said, grinning at him.

Ginny and Dan, the other two Pirates, met them at the gates.

'You'd better watch out. Craig is looking for you,' Ginny warned him.

'You'll have to keep out of the way

for a bit,' Dan said.

'That's what I told him,' Josie put in. 'What we've got to do is find out where Craig is all the time and make sure Jason is somewhere else.'

The bell went without Craig being seen. They went into the classroom. Some boys told Jason that Craig was going to get him, but he didn't feel so bad knowing that the Pirates were on his side.

In assembly he saw Craig for the first time.

He couldn't stop his eyes searching the top classes to see if Craig was in school. When their eyes met, Craig made threatening faces at him. He tried to look puzzled, as though he didn't under-stand why there should be any quarrel between them.

The morning's lessons seemed to flash by. He could stay in the library at break, but at dinner-time everyone had to go outside and he would be at Craig's mercy.

The last lesson of the morning was number work. Jason took his cards and book up to Mrs Shaw. The frightened feeling was in his stomach again.

'Can I have some cards, miss, to catch up?' he asked, before he knew what he was going to say.

'You mean to take home?' Mrs Shaw asked.

'I thought I could stay in at dinner-time and do the ones I should've done yesterday.' He tried to keep his voice calm.

'This is not like you, Jason – I'm pleased

to say.' She took another two cards out of the box. 'You can see how far you get with these.'

'Thank you, miss.' Jason returned to his seat. 'That's dinner-hour safe,' he whispered to Josie.

'If you keep out of Craig's way today, he might forget about you. Tomorrow's Saturday. By Monday he'll probably have got over it,' Josie said encouragingly. 'We'll try to find out at dinner-time what he's planning. Don't worry, the Pirates are with you.'

'Thanks,' Jason said. Josie always understood how the others felt.

The bell went and everyone rushed out. Jason did a bit of work then looked out of the window. He saw Craig and his slaves. They were searching for someone – him.

He was being hunted. He felt trapped. He couldn't eat much of his packed lunch. The sick feeling came again. He could see no way to escape being beaten up. Really beaten up. Not just the sort of scuffle he could get out of, but punches in the face. He sat hunched up at his desk.

When the bell went, he jumped. There was no need for the Pirates to find out what Craig was planning, because when the class came in Alistair brought a message.

'Craig says to tell you,' he repeated as though reciting a poem in assembly, 'that he'll be waiting for you after school.'

'Let him wait as long as he likes,' Ginny snapped.

'Are you going to help me this time?' Jason asked Alistair. He was sorry as soon as he spoke. He was just taking it out on

Alistair because he felt helpless.

'You should not have bent his spokes,' Alistair said. 'That was not necessary.'

Jason ignored him. No one understood Alistair. Sometimes he sounded like a grown-up, at other times like a little kid.

There was football last thing that after-noon.

'When we finish, you want to get changed quick and clear off. I would,' Josie said, looking worried.

'I couldn't get home before Craig caught up with me on his bike, even if I ran all the way. I'm not as fast as you.'

'Does he know where you live?' Josie asked.

Jason nodded miserably. 'I think so.'

'What you could do is go home by Long Lane,' Dan suggested. 'If you get out before anyone else, you'd be out of sight and he wouldn't know where you'd gone.'

Long Lane was a winding road which made a loop on his usual way home.

'I could do that,' Jason said. He felt better again. Even if Craig caught him, he wouldn't feel so bad knowing that the Pirates were on his side. He had friends; Craig only had slaves.

'You'll have to get changed quick,' Josie said. She suddenly felt furious with Craig. It wasn't right for him to pick on people the way he did. 'I hate Craig!' she burst out. She was usually the calmest of the Pirates and the others went quiet with surprise.

'I hate Craig as well,' a girl called Mandy, who was standing near them, said. 'He's just a bully.'

'I thought you were a friend of his,' Jason answered.

'I was once, but I got sick of him. He's scared really, that's why he makes younger kids do things. He nearly got my cousin Tim killed.'

'What did he do?' Ginny asked.

'He made Tim climb down the cliff to look for gulls' eggs. Tim got stuck, and Craig wouldn't help him. So I gave him a push to make him help – we were miles from the edge – and he started yelling. He was really scared and wouldn't go near the edge. He was shaking he was so frightened.'

'I'm not surprised,' Josie said. 'That's just what he would do.'

As soon as football finished, Jason ran. He broke the school rule about not leaving before the bell and was out two minutes early. He didn't slow down until he was out of sight along Long Lane.

Then came the difficult part. Just waiting. He had to let enough time go by for Craig to think he had got home.

Jason suddenly felt angry. He would not become a slave. A slave always had to do what someone else wanted. He looked around at the strange road. What was he doing here?

He told himself to walk on and never mind if he did bump into Craig. But he was still too afraid. His body didn't do what he told it – just like a slave's.

When he thought that he'd waited long enough, he began to walk again. At the end of the lane he stopped and looked along his road in both directions. It was empty.

He marched happily forward. It was only a hundred yards to his house on the other side of the road. He'd made it! The overgrown hedges and the tall, old gate posts at the ends of the drives welcomed him home.

Craig stepped out from behind the gate post of the first drive he came to. Jason's only thought was that it wasn't fair.

CHAPTER THREE

Beaten – But Not Defeated!

'I want you, Jason Peter Smith,' Craig said coldly.

His face was white with anger. Jason saw that Craig was one of those boys who could make himself angry when he wanted.

'Hello,' Jason said. 'What for?' He tried to sound interested but his throat was dry

and his voice croaked.

'You know what for. Do you know how much what you did cost, you stupid little kid?'

'D'you mean the bike? I'll pay for that,'

Jason offered, feeling his knees trembling.

'You'll pay all right,' Craig told him, coming nearer.

Jason backed into the hedge. There was no one about. They were hidden from the houses and he was at Craig's mercy.

Craig walked right up to him and punched him on the nose. It began to run or bleed, he didn't know which. His eyes watered so that he couldn't see clearly. He blinked, trying not to cry. His nose felt hot and cold at the same time.

'Thought you could escape me, did you?'

'No,' Jason said. 'I'm sorry.'

'I'll make you sorry all right.' Craig hit him again, this time in the mouth.

Jason's lips suddenly felt huge, as though they covered half his face. He didn't know what to do.

'You're going to be sorry you ever got smart with me.' Craig hit him on the side of his head by his eye. It began to throb.

Jason tried to shield himself but didn't dare hit back for fear of making Craig angrier.

He stopped a punch with his bag and made Craig graze his knuckles.

'You're going to learn a lesson you won't forget.'

Craig swung wildly. Punches showered onto Jason's shoulders. They didn't hurt so much after the others. He hid his head behind his bag and sank into the hedge. Someone must come along the road soon, was all he could think.

After a minute, Craig stopped.

Jason kept his bag up. Nothing will ever be the same again, he kept saying to

himself. Nothing will ever be the same
again.

His face throbbed with pain.

'Had enough?' Craig demanded.

Jason blinked away the tears which filled
his eyes. He had not cried. In spite of all
the punches, he had not cried.

He lowered his bag and looked at Craig.
Jason saw that the anger Craig had built up
had gone.

Suddenly Jason found he wasn't afraid
any more. He felt angry again. He would
not be a slave.

'Had enough?' Craig asked again.

'Never,' he replied. It was difficult to
make his lips move to speak. His voice
sounded thick.

He stared at Craig without blinking and
saw something else. For a moment he

wasn't sure what it was. Then he was sure: Craig did not know what to do next. He had not thought about anything more than hitting him.

Jason stared without saying anything else and saw something even more puzzling. He saw that Craig was afraid.

That did it. It was as if something inside Jason went click.

'What're you afraid of, Craig?' he demanded through swollen lips.

Jason shrugged himself out of the hedge, slung his bag from his shoulder and pushed past Craig. For some reason, Craig let him go.

Jason knew that he would never be afraid of Craig again. No one had ever hit him like that before. His face felt like a tender, throbbing, sore balloon – but he no longer feared Craig. If that was the worst he could do, he could take it. He felt free. He would never be Craig's slave, nor anyone else's.

He went home with a swelling eye, split lips and blood from his nose dripping down his shirt. But he was definitely not defeated. Not this time.

CHAPTER FOUR

Family Surprises

Jason decided to try to get into the house without being seen. He ran down his secret path between the bushes and the fence until he was opposite the back door.

He thought he would sneak upstairs, clean his face up, put on his jeans and T-shirt and then nobody would know what

had happened. That would save a lot of
fuss. He could explain away the blood by
saying that his nose kept bleeding after
football – which was true, in one way.

He made it to the bathroom without
being heard. When he saw his face in the
mirror, he knew that his idea of keeping

quiet about the fight was impossible. One eye was purple and his lips were swollen and split.

He washed gently. Everything stung or throbbed. He wondered if he would ever feel normal again. He got changed and went downstairs. His mother was in the kitchen.

She had just taken a dish out of the oven. When she saw him, she made a great show of putting it down extra carefully.

She looked at him before speaking. 'What has happened?' she asked quietly.

Jason decided it would be best to tell everything quickly. 'I had a fight,' he said, trying to sound as though that was what he usually said when he got home.

'I can see that,' his mother said. 'Who was the fight with?'

Jason mumbled something.

'Who?'

'A boy.'

His mother looked· at him as though wondering whether she could force him to tell her who.

'Was he bigger than you?'

Jason nodded.

'How old was he?'

'I don't know exactly.'

'Older than you?'

'A bit.'

'At your school?'

'Umm.'

'Do you know which year?'

'Yes.'

'Well, which?'

'The top,' Jason mumbled.

'He can't be allowed to do this sort of thing,' she said grimly.

'What are you going to do?' Jason asked, getting worried.

'We shall speak to the headmistress.'

'No. Don't, please.'

'Why did he pick on you?'

Jason thought for a moment. He had half an idea at the back of his mind.

'I pushed him off his bike.'

'You know what you've been told about fighting.'

Jason looked at the floor.

'We'll discuss this with your father when he comes in.' She went to the cupboard where the TCP and cotton wool were kept. 'Come here and I'll clean you up.'

'I've done that already.'

'Put this towel round you.' He shuffled slowly forward. 'Quickly – if you want any dinner tonight.'

Everything started to sting again. It was worse when someone else was doing the dabbing.

Jason waited anxiously for his father to come home from work. He was sure to get some punishment. He tried to guess what.

When his father came in, he was sitting in front of the television but not really looking at it.

'Hello,' Jason said, trying yet again that day to sound normal.

'I hear you've been in a fight,' his father said, as though he wouldn't have known if he'd not been told.

'Yes.'

'You started it, did you?'

Jason nodded. 'Well. . .' he started to explain, but his father went on.

'I hope you've learnt your lesson,' he said seriously.

'Umm,' Jason agreed.

'You know what we've told you about fighting?'

Jason nodded again. 'Are you going to tell the school?'

'That's something I'll have to think about,' his father said, frowning. 'Yes, I'll think about that,' he repeated, and then left him to watch the television.

Suddenly Jason knew that he wasn't going to get into trouble. He was so surprised that he forgot about his bruised face for almost half a minute.

Jason and Mark were allowed to have their dinner in front of the television. 'So that they can talk about you,' Mark told him.

Jason found eating difficult. His lips did not stretch properly.

'D'you think they'll tell the school?'

'No, of course not. They can't since you said you started it.'

Jason smiled. His lips stung sharply. 'I didn't exactly say that.'

'Anyway, Dad's rather proud of you, though he can't show it.'

'Oh.' Jason was surprised again.

'Who did it?' Mark asked in a different voice.

'Craig Sullivan. D'you know him?'

'His brother is at High School with us. He was always picking on younger kids until Jamie Cole gave him a good thumping. He's all right now.'

'I see,' Jason said.

'D'you want us to get Craig?'

'No, thanks.'
'I could tell him to leave you alone.'
'It's all right.'
'Okay. But if he does it again, I will.'
Jason went to bed that night with his face

throbbing, but what interested him more was how his family had behaved. It had not been how he had expected – and he felt quite shocked that his family could surprise him.

It had been a funny day, he thought, before he fell asleep. Besides getting beaten up, he had learned something about himself, about his family and about bullies.

CHAPTER FIVE

The Coombe Bay Pirates

The next morning, as happened most Saturdays, the Pirates met at their boat-shed den to decide how to spend the day. It was made of planks and beams from old boats, and the cracks were filled with tar. It belonged to Josie's parents but they no longer used it since they'd built a new

concrete one.

The Pirates' boatshed stood at the top
of the beach just above the high-tide mark,
and they could hear the waves like back-
ground music at all their meetings. It was

filled with things they had found on the beach: planks, shells, odd-shaped stones, bits of rope off boats, and four lobster pots on which they sat when they held meetings.

When Jason arrived, the others gazed in amazement at his battered face.

Ginny whistled in surprise. She had curly fair hair and was the biggest of the Pirates. She also had a fierce temper which the others were careful of. 'I've never seen an eye that colour,' she exclaimed.

'Does it hurt much?' Dan asked.

'Not if I don't touch it.'

'Did you get into trouble?' Ginny asked.

'Not really. They just made me promise not to fight.'

'You were lucky,' Ginny said. 'When I got in a fight, I wasn't allowed out for two weeks.'

'They said there were better ways of settling arguments than by fighting,' Jason told them.

'They always say that,' Josie said.

'If you ask them what those ways are,' Dan put in, 'they never tell you any you can really use.' The others nodded. Dan was tall and gangly and easily the cleverest of the Pirates, but he usually did what the others suggested.

'They tell you to sort things out by talking,' Josie said.

'Huh!' Jason exclaimed. 'Craig didn't look to me as though he wanted a chat.'

'How did he get you?' Ginny asked. 'We thought you'd got away.'

'When Craig came out,' Josie added, 'we told him you were still getting changed from football.'

'But then one of his slaves in our class said you'd already gone,' Ginny said angrily.

'He was waiting in a gateway by my house.' Jason described how he'd been caught. 'It was too late when I saw him.'

'Did you hit him much?' Ginny wanted to know.

'Not really.'

'We'll have to think of some way to get him.' Ginny pressed her lips together.

'Right,' Dan said, 'let's have a proper meeting to work out what we're going to do.'

They sat in a circle on their lobster pots.

'We could slip out one night and go over to Craig's house and let his bike tyres down or loosen his brakes,' Ginny suggested. 'He'd think it was burglars.'

'We don't want to kill him,' Josie said quickly.

'Who doesn't?' Ginny snorted.

'Burglars don't sabotage bikes, anyway,' Dan pointed out.

'He'd guess who it was,' Jason added, 'and I don't want to get beaten up again, thank you very much.'

'Well, you think of something. It's for you we're doing it.' Ginny let her shoulders drop and blew out her breath as though she was going to sulk.

'It's not just for Jason we're doing it,' Josie said. She pushed her glasses up her nose. 'When we became Pirates, we said we'd help each other. So it's for all of us.'

'For everyone really, not just us,' Dan said thoughtfully. 'Craig's got to be stopped from doing it again.'

'Well, how?' Ginny asked, coming back to life.

'I don't know,' Dan said, shaking his head.

'We won't do anything, as usual,' she said, letting her shoulders droop again.

'We've got to think of something,' Josie said, almost begging the others to.

'We will this time,' Jason promised her.

They looked at his battered face. He was always untidy. His ordinary brown hair seemed to stick out whatever he did, and his mother told him to tidy himself up every time she saw him. Now his bruised and puffed-up face made him look even more of a mess. He would have looked defeated as well, but there was something about him which was determined. It was usually Jason who had the ideas, but he didn't have any just then.

'What're we going to do today?' Ginny

asked at last.

The Pirates sat on their lobster pots and thought. But it was not a good morning for ideas.

CHAPTER SIX

Rescuing Alistair

On Monday Jason went to school as usual. His face was back to normal except for a black eye. Mrs Shaw wanted to know what had happened. He mumbled about having had a bit of a fight, and tried to make it sound like nothing much. 'It wasn't at school,' he added.

Mrs Shaw snorted, as though she thought there was more going on than Jason was telling her, but all she said was, 'I shall be keeping an eye on you from now on, Jason Smith, and it won't be a funny coloured

one like yours.'

The dinner-hour was nearly over when Jason came up against Craig again. The Pirates were wandering round the school field when they heard voices behind the caretaker's hut. It sounded as though there was a fight going on.

'Let's go and see,' Ginny suggested.

They ran round and found Alistair standing against the side of the hut. Four of Craig's slaves were stopping his escape. Craig himself was doing nothing except urging them on. He was sitting on a pile of wood like someone with the best seat at a circus.

'Let me go past,' Alistair begged and tried to step forward. One of the slaves pushed him back.

'All you've got to do,' Craig told him, 'is go the other way – over the hut.'

Those who were watching had guilty looks on their faces. The noise was coming from Craig's slaves.

'Leave him alone,' Josie shouted as soon as she saw what was happening.

Alistair had tears in his eyes.

'Let him go,' Jason said to one of the slaves.

'Clear off, Jason,' the boy replied. 'Unless you want another black eye.'

He looked at the others for a laugh.

Jason jumped forward and punched him hard on the top of his arm. The boy was so surprised he gave a yell and clutched his shoulder without trying to hit back.

Dan, who was no good at fighting, aimed a kick at one of the others. His foot caught the boy just under his knee and he fell on the grass with a squeal. He rolled about, holding his leg. Dan was more amazed than anyone.

Josie gave one of the last two a push. Her face looked so furious he jumped back in fright.

'He can go,' the last slave said quickly, as Ginny went towards him. 'It was only a bit of fun.'

Ginny, the strongest of the Pirates, shoved the boy against the shed but didn't do anything else.

Craig put on a smile which was supposed to tell everyone that he was enjoying the show.

Jason turned to him. 'What're you scared of, Craig? Why don't you pick on someone your own size?'

'This was nothing to do with me,' Craig laughed. 'You'd have another bleeding

nose by now if it had been, Jason Peter
Smith.'

'Come on,' Jason said to Alistair.

They walked away.

It was at that moment that Jason remem-
bered something and had his idea for
stopping Craig.

CHAPTER SEVEN

The Pirates and the School Bully

On a Monday afternoon the usual school routine was changed. Two classes were put together: some children went for extra reading, while others had a choice of activities. This was the Pirates' chance to put their plan into action.

Josie, who could put on a very innocent

face, told Mrs Shaw that they were going to the library to choose books. What she didn't say was that on the way there they had something else to do. They tried to look as normal as possible when they left the classroom.

Once they were in the corridor, Josie let out her breath and breathed again. 'Phew!' She pushed her glasses up her nose. 'My face felt all funny when I said we were going to the library. I thought she'd guess we were up to something.'

'You were great,' Jason told her.

'Come on, we'd better be quick,' Dan said, looking worried.

They made sure no one was in the corridor, then slipped quickly out a side door.

A few seconds later they were round the back of the school hall by the bicycle sheds,

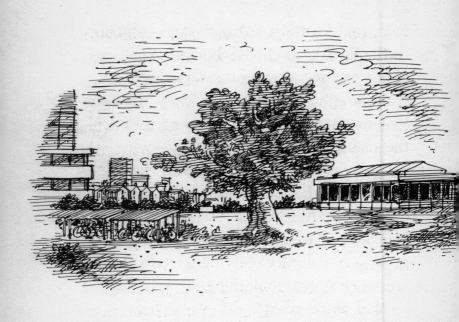

where an immensely long ladder was kept.

'Are you sure no one can see us here?' Josie asked.

'No. We're all right,' Jason said, trying not to sound as nervous as he felt.

'Come on then,' Ginny said, wanting to do something because she had suddenly got a fluttering feeling in her stomach.

The Pirates got hold of the ladder and carried it out into the space between the school hall and the bicycle shed. A huge oak tree grew behind the shed and pointed a long branch like an arm towards the school.

It took all the Pirates' strength to stand the ladder up straight, and then they found it would not do what they wanted. It seemed to be alive and fighting them.

'Go slowly,' Ginny grunted as they started to lean it towards the branch. The ladder wobbled. 'Don't push.'

'I'm not,' Josie and Dan answered together as it dragged them forward. 'It's pulling us.'

'I can't hold it,' Jason gasped.

The ladder tore itself from their hands and smashed through leaves and twigs before crashing into the branch.

The noise seemed like a thunderstorm right overhead.

The Pirates froze. Four horrified faces gaped at each other. They seemed unable to move. Josie had stopped breathing. Ginny's arms were stuck out in front of her as though still holding the ladder. Jason's face was throbbing again. Dan could feel his heart beating. Anyone coming round the corner would have found four statues.

Jason came back to life first. 'No one's coming,' he panted.

'They must have heard,' Josie gasped.

'It's all right,' Dan said, starting to think again. 'People never take any notice of bangs outside if they can't see anything.

And no one can see us here.'

Josie shook her head as though she couldn't believe it.

'We'd better not waste time,' Ginny said.

'You get the rope,' Jason ordered. 'Josie, keep a look out just in case anyone does come to see what the noise was. Dan, help me get his bike.' The Pirates scattered.

Jason and Dan came back carrying Craig's bike, which had a padlock and chain on its front wheel.

Ginny returned from the caretaker's hut with a rope. 'Is this long enough, do you think?' she asked.

'It looks it,' Jason said. 'I'll take one end and you pay it out as I climb.'

Josie called, 'All clear still,' from the corner of the hall.

Jason started to climb the ladder. As he went up, it bent and swayed. He kept his eyes on the branch above and dragged the rope after him. At the top, he pushed it over the branch and caught hold of the end.

When he looked down to speak to the others, the ground seemed miles away. He clutched the ladder to stop himself falling and breathed deeply. The empty space seemed to be pulling at him. Keep looking up at the branch, he told himself.

'Okay,' he called, without looking at them. His throat felt dry.

Ginny tied the rope under the handlebars of the bike.

'Go on!' Dan called.

Jason pulled and nearly fell off the ladder.

'Lift it up as high as you can,' he called down.

'Come and help,' Ginny hissed at Josie.

The three of them raised the bike to arm's length above their heads.

Carefully, Jason tucked one arm through the rungs of the ladder and began to pull. The bike rose slowly into the air. He pulled the rope steadily, hand over hand, until the bike hit the branch. Then he wedged his shoulder against the ladder and held the rope with one hand. There was a sawn-off branch near his head. He made a loop of rope and slipped it over the stump. To stop it slipping, he wound the rope round it a few more times.

Quickly, he pulled up the loose rope and piled it on top of the main branch. He climbed down. His hands were wet with sweat and his knees felt wobbly, but not in the same way as when he had been trapped by Craig.

The Pirates stood back to admire their work. High above their heads, Craig's bike swung gently in the breeze.

'D'you think it will work?' Josie whispered.

'If what Mandy said is right, it will,' Dan said firmly.

'We've got him!' Ginny growled.

'Do you think we really should do this?' Josie wondered.

'He's got to be stopped,' Dan said.

'He deserves it,' Ginny agreed.

Josie still looked doubtful.

'Come on,' Jason said.

They ran to the library and took four books. Then they hurried back to their classroom, trying to look normal.

When the bell went for the end of the day, they dashed back to the cycle shed to put their plan into action. As the cyclists came to collect their bikes, a crowd gathered. No one went home. Craig's bike turned slowly in the air, like bait at the end of a fishing line.

At last Craig arrived. His face lit up when he saw the crowd, as though he expected a fight to be going on. Then he saw his bicycle and knew that the centre of the circle was being kept for him. His face turned white.

'Funny place to park your bike, Craig,' an unknown voice called out.

'Who's done that?' he demanded. His voice went squeaky.

'Don't know,' several voices sang out.

Some boys from Craig's year arrived.

'Hey, Craig, can your bike fly?' one called out.

'It can do anything – it's got a fixed wheel,' another voice replied.

'Where's it fixed?'

'Up a tree.'

Everyone laughed. Jason was surprised to find that Craig was not as popular as he had always thought. His lips stung as he smiled.

Craig turned on him, seeing him grinning. 'Did you do this, Jason?'

'I learnt my lesson, didn't I?' Jason replied.

'I didn't know bikes could climb trees!' someone behind Craig shouted.

He turned round but was too late to see who.

'Let's see you fly it, Craig,' another

voice said.

Craig turned to one of his slaves.

'Go up the ladder and lower it down slowly,' he ordered.

'Get it yourself,' the slave replied, stepping back into the crowd.

'What're you scared of, Craig?' Jason asked.

'Craig's chicken,' a voice sounding like Dan's said loudly.

'Cluck, cluck, cluck,' a voice sounding like Ginny's added.

'What're you scared of?' Jason asked again.

Others took up the cry. 'Craig's scared. Craig's scared.'

'All right, I will,' Craig said, his eyes very wide.

Something made the circle of watchers

fall silent.

Craig began to climb the ladder. He kept gazing up at his bike. His face was white. He looked, Jason thought, like one of the statues in the cemetery.

The ladder bent like a springboard as he climbed higher.

'D'you think we ought to get a teacher?' Josie whispered.

'Not yet,' Dan said, keeping his eyes on Craig.

When he was a few rungs from the top, the ladder gave a shudder and slid an inch along the branch.

Craig's fear of heights took hold of him just as it had that time near the cliff edge, which Mandy had told them about.

He flattened himself against the rungs and gave a frightened cry. He looked through the ladder at the circle of faces below. 'I can't move!' he cried. 'I can't move. I'm going to fall.' His voice became a sob.

'Now we ought to get someone,' Dan said.

At that moment, Mr Evans came to see why no cyclists had left the school.

'Keep still!' he shouted, pushing his way through the circle.

'I'm going to fall!' Craig moaned.

'No, you're not,' Mr Evans told him calmly. 'I've got the ladder. Now just put your left leg on the rung below.'

'I can't move!' Craig cried again.

'Yes, you can,' Mr Evans promised him. 'You won't fall.'

'I can't move!' Craig said again, his voice rising.

'All right,' Mr Evans said. 'I'll tell you
what we'll do. I'll come up and help you.'
'No!' Craig shrieked. 'Don't touch me.'
Mr Evans ignored him and climbed slowly
up the ladder. Rung by rung he brought

Craig down, talking quietly to him all the way.

By the time Craig reached the ground his days as a bully were over. Jason's victory was complete. But he found to his surprise that he felt sorry for Craig. When he thought about it, it couldn't be much fun only having slaves instead of friends.

'That's fixed him,' Ginny said softly.

'Come on, let's go,' Josie said.

'Stand still!' Mr Evans shouted. 'Who did this?'

No one said anything.

'Did any of you think what might have happened?' Mr Evans demanded. 'I want whoever did this to come to see me first thing in the morning.'

Mr Evans led Craig away. He was still shaking.

'Do you think we should own up?' Ginny asked.

'Yes, we ought to,' Josie decided for all of them.

'I don't want to get into trouble,' Jason said.

'It's not just you,' Ginny reminded him. 'We'll all go to see Mr Evans.'

'I don't think we will get into much trouble,' Dan said thoughtfully. 'Not when he knows why we did it.'

The Pirates walked slowly out of school.

Jason frowned. 'It's funny. Now we've won, I don't feel like jumping up and down.'

'I know what you mean,' Josie agreed. 'Perhaps we shouldn't have done it '

'Still, it should stop him,' Ginny said.

Dan looked worried. 'I hope so.'

'All you've really got to do with a bully,'

Jason said, 'is not be afraid of him.'

Ginny gave him a push which sent him into the hedge. 'Let's race to the pick-and-mix shop. I've got some money.'

The Coombe Bay Pirates charged down the road. Josie won as usual, and Jason was last as always.

'We're free!' he shouted, as he crashed into the others.

YOUR GUESS IS AS GOOD AS MINE

by BERNARD ASHLEY
Illustrated by DAVID PARKINS

The rain hit Nicky hard as he came out of school and everyone ran. It was screams and running feet all along the street, especially when the thunder started. So it seemed too good to be true when he saw his Dad's yellow Mini. But it wasn't his Dad's car, nor was it his Dad driving and Nicky is suddenly plunged into a terrifying adventure and a frantic race against time . . .

0 552 524506

THE BIG MATCH

by ROB CHILDS
Illustrated by TIM MORWOOD

'ACE SAVE, CHRIS!' shouted Andrew as his younger brother pushed yet another of his best shots round the post. 'You're unbeatable today.'

But will he be unbeatable when he is picked to stand in for the regular school team goalkeeper in a vital cup game against Shenby School, their main rivals? For Chris is several years younger than the rest of the team – and they aren't all as sure of his skill in goal as his older brother is . . .

A fast-moving and realistic footballing story for young readers.

0 552 524727

MIKE'S MAGIC SEEDS

by ALEXANDER McCALL SMITH
Illustrated by KATE SHANNON

When Mike buys a strange packet of seeds
with the last of his pocket money, he is
amazed to discover that they grow into the
most wonderful plants – each one produces
a different kind of sweet! Suddenly Mike is
very popular at school.

But then nosy Angela starts asking
awkward questions. If Mike isn't careful,
she might discover his secret and ruin
everything . . .

0 552 52476X

THE BIG OLD HORSE

by EVELYN DAVIES
Illustrated by TERRY RILEY

Oh, what a commotion when the fair arrived! The big old horse leaned over the hedge to have a look – and got quite a shock. PINK SPOTTED HORSES! Yellow and green and red and mauve horses!

He was curious, then frightened, then jealous when the little boy down the lane, so excited by the fair, forgot to come and feed him. Worst of all, the farmer then came along and chained him up. Why? What had he done wrong? He was very upset . . .

But when disaster struck the fair, it was the big old horse who came to the rescue and made sure all the children had a wonderful day!

0 552 524719

THE KILLER TADPOLE

by JACQUELINE WILSON
Illustrated by LESLEY SMITH

'Do you want to be in my gang?' Spike hissed.

Well, Spike was very good at bashing people up, so how could Nicholas refuse? But, to join the gang, he has to undergo three Terrible Ordeals.

To Nicholas's amazement, one of the Ordeals ends with a big surprise – a tadpole that keeps growing, and growing, and growing until it becomes what must be the largest tadpole in the world – the Killer Tadpole! Perhaps it can save him from Spike – and from getting bashed up!

0 552 52414X

If you would like to receive a Newsletter about our new Children's books, just fill in the coupon below with your name and address (or copy it onto a separate piece of paper if you don't want to spoil your book) and send it to:

The Children's Books Editor
Young Corgi Books
61-63 Uxbridge Road,
Ealing
London W5 5SA

Please send me a Children's Newsletter:

Name. H e L e n   D u n n

Address.

All Children's Books are available at your bookshop or newsagent, or can be ordered from the following address:
Corgi/Bantam Books,
Cash Sales Department,
P.O. Box 11, Falmouth, Cornwall TR10 9 EN

Please send a cheque or postal order (no currency) and allow 60p for postage and packing for the first book plus 25p for the second book and 15p for each additional book ordered up to a maximum charge of £1.90 in UK.

B.F.P.O. customers please allow 60p for the first book, 25p for the second book plus 15p per copy for the next 7 books, thereafter 9p per book.

Overseas customers, including Eire, please allow £1.25 for postage and packing for the first book, 75p for the second book, and 28p for each subsequent title ordered.